The Calico Jungle

THE CALICO

Alfred A. Knopf ~ New York

JUNGLE

written and illustrated by

Dahlov Ipcar

L. C. Catalog card number: 65–21557

THIS IS A BORZOI BOOK, PUBLISHED BY ALFRED A. KNOPF, INC.

For Barbara Emily,
who plays with calico animals and sleeps on a tiger-skin rug

Once there was a little boy whose mother
made him a wonderful calico quilt for his bed.
It was a beautiful quilt, all covered with
jungle trees and flowers and animals.

Every night, after his mother tucked him
into bed and kissed him good night,
the little boy lay there in his bed, in the
dim evening light, and looked at all the animals
among the strange and wonderful trees.

Under the trees, calico flowers grew and calico butterflies
flew. And there were peacocks and rabbits there.

Some of the animals were not easy to see. The little boy
had to look hard to see the black-and-white zebras
hiding among the tree trunks.

And he had to look carefully to see
the coily, spotted snake winding its way
through a tree full of flowers and fruits.

There were tall giraffes hiding there,
with their heads above the treetops,
eating leaves.

High in the treetops calico squirrels
climbed about eating nuts.

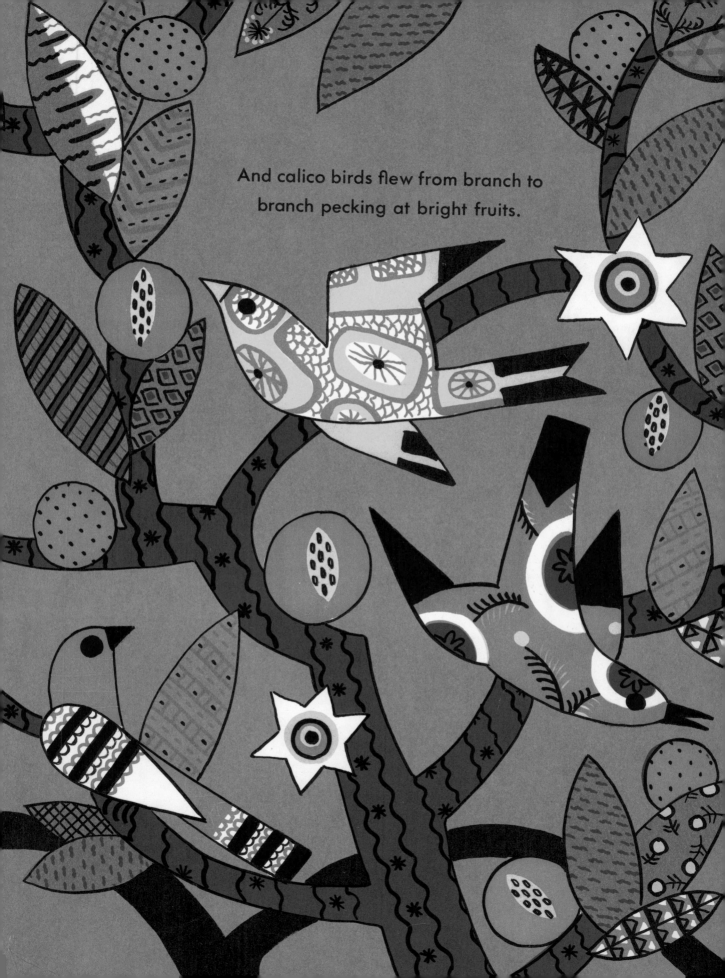

And calico birds flew from branch to branch pecking at bright fruits.

Some of the animals were easy to see,
such as a white unicorn and a big black rhinoceros
—each with one long horn.

Grazing among the trees were wild antelopes with long horns.

Some of them were running away
to hide in the depths of the jungle.

And, in the very middle of the jungle, was a lovely, deep green pool.

There, big black elephants gave each other shower baths.

Fish swam in the pool,
calico fish with strange shapes
and bright colors, shining like jewels
in the rippling green water.

Fat black hippos splashed in the pool,
and big green crocodiles swam there.

Long-legged birds waded in the water, catching fish.

And all the animals came to the pool to drink.

And, deeper in the jungle, beyond the pool,
where it was quiet and dark and peaceful,
the little boy found a sleeping lion and a sleeping tiger,
and a small jungle cat
asleep under a bush.

And further on, a camel and a spotted horse were sleeping side by side under a big calico tree.

And a small spotted dog was
curled up tight in a sleepy ball.

All the animals were asleep at the far end of
the quilt and, by the time the little boy had
explored that far, he was growing sleepy, too.
He closed his eyes, and then he fell asleep and
dreamed that he was walking through the calico
jungle, under the flowering trees, where all the
strange and wonderful animals lived.

Text set in Futura Medium. Composed at Westcott & Thomson, Philadelphia, Pennsylvania. Printed by Reehl Litho, New York City. Bound by Economy Bookbinding Corp., Kearny, New Jersey.